AMAZONIN

by David ____

DEDICATION

This book is dedicated to my good friend Katie Fyfe and her daughter Grace.

AMAZONING GRACE

CONTENTS

Page No.

CHAPTERS

AMAZONING GRACE

Chapter One

THE WAYS OF DREAMING

No-one actually knows where dreams come. It is equally true in exactly the same way that there is no human alive or dead who can be sure with any degree of certainty where dreams end up once they are finished with. That is just the way it is!

This is a tale about a very particular dream that was experienced by a very particular girl named Grace Fyfe. Before you start reading the dramatic account of the events that flooded into her sleeping mind it should be made perfectly clear that some parts of the story are scary indeed and other aspects are decidedly odd.

It is the way of dreams that very often the sleeping minds of those involved have a deeper level of consciousness running parallel to the events of the dream itself. They are aware that what they are encountering is not a true reality and that they can awake at any time.

Whilst there is an element of fear and anxiety involved the dreamer is at all times aware that what they are experiencing is not actually happening and that it will all be over soon. So that is a relief to everyone concerned.

Not so very long ago it was widely believed that people would have bad dreams if they ate too much cheese late at night. That explanation sounds just a little bit silly now. Today there are lots of "experts" all over the world who will propose all manner of notions of what dreams actually are and will provide plausible suggestions to intemperate the secrets of what they really mean.

You know they cannot all be right. In fact, it is far more likely that they are all entirely wrong, because experts are just people who come up with explanations that seem good enough until another expert comes along with a different idea that disproves whatever notion it is that they are proposing.

As you will know, it is not the way of humans to say "we do not understand what this thing is, it is a mystery", and then simply leave it alone. Humans were created with inquiring minds and always think that they have to know everything.

Other animals on the planet are quite happy to go on living their lives not bothering too much about the way of dreams, they just carry on in their own particular ways quite happily oblivious to concerns about psychology and the secret workings of the mind and issues around consciousness and different levels of sleep.

You will never find a goat or a ladybird reading a book by a clever Austrian man telling them what it means if they spent the night dreaming about what it was like having two extra sets of legs. There was never an earwig born that ever concerned him or herself too much if they had spent the entire night dreaming that they were made of concrete. No, it is the way of dreams that they are mysteries and that is quite simply just the way they were always meant to be.

Now this young Grace child was actually not a naughty girl. She did occasionally do things that seemed naughty. For example, there was that time when she threw her cushion out of the window of the car when it was traveling along the motorway. But that was an accidental type of naughtiness.

Grace was not one of those girls who was sometimes deliberately naughty. In actual fact she was one of those children who adults really liked because she was always very polite and even tempered and seemed very kind. In times gone by she would have been called "sweet natured" but that is not a term that you hear used very much nowadays, even though children are almost certainly just as sweet as they have always been.

There are a couple of things that you probably should know about Grace and her way of life at the start of this story because there is a big difference between things that are facts and things that are imagined. So the first absolute fact we know for certain is that her mother was called Katie. Now Katie was probably an inch or two shorter than average, she had shoulder length blond hair and most people would describe her as being a very bright and attractive woman.

She was hard working and had excellent principles and had always made sure that Grace was aware of the difference between right and wrong. Katie was also very protective of her daughter and also very proud of her. They got on very well together and would happily chat and play together. Katie did all the adult things and that allowed Grace to be a child and to grow up in a very happy sort of way.

Steve was the name of Grace's father and he was a man who liked to exercise and was very strong and fit. He ha a job that kept him very busy but Grace was not exactly sure what type of work he did. Perhaps it had something to do with building sites?

Then there were various grandparents and uncles and aunts and cousins and all manner of friends who formed the wider family circle. So we see that young Grace was growing up in an way that was very protected and she always felt very safe. So it was perhaps a surprise that her dream took her to a place where she was vulnerable. In her real life she had never felt that way.

One fact that the story neglects to mention is that there were actually two dogs living in the family home at the time this story takes place. There was a lovely older dog who had given birth to six puppies last Christmas. Five of these were taken into new homes among the rest of the family but the youngest of the litter,

Reggie, had stayed and was happily growing up with Grace as his constant companion. They were just devoted to each other.

So are you ready. Our story starts when Grace was in her bed all curled up warmly snuggled beneath her duvet. All the day she had been playing with her friends from school on her trampoline in the garden and was pretty much as bounced out as any normal eight-year-old girl could be. Somewhere by the side of her bed Reggie the puppy was already starting to snore gently.

You can never really be certain of the thoughts that run through your mind in the moments before you doze off into deeper sleep. Perhaps Grace was just thinking about the school work project the class were involved with were they were all learning all about the environment. However, it might just as easily have been another matter that was completely divorced from what happened next. The world of dreams is far from a precise science.

Grace had her eyes closed and her mind just drifted off into the night, in the same way that happens to all of us every night. Our daytime thoughts just dissolve into nothingness and whatever happens next is just the way things are meant to be. Who knows what happens when our eyes are closed and our minds become linked together with strange uninvited thoughts.

Chapter Two

A SUDDEN BUMP

Grace had mixed feelings about tarantulas. On one hand they were really quite fascinating. Yet she knew that they could also be very dangerous and needed to be treated with the greatest possible respect. Now because Grace was a very well behaved and clever eight-year-old girl she was always very careful when she came across a a potentially lethal arachnid. However, her puppy Reggie did not really understand the dangerous nature of the world's most poisonous spider and so Grace needed to be especially vigilant on his behalf.

Really Grace and Reggie should not have been left wondering around in the Amazon rain forest by themselves. It really is not the sort of place where a child and a puppy should be fending for themselves. However sometimes unexpected things happen to even the most careful of people and very often that is how adventures begin.

Time seemed to pass in a very different way over in the backwaters of Brazil. For what she felt seem like the past ten days Grace and her parents and the puppy had been slowly drifting along in wonderment and awe as they meandered deeper and deeper into the heart of the rain forest. Above them there were always brightly coloured bird flitting around and chasing each other in their wild games.

There were as many different types of birds as you could possibly imagine. Graces favourite was the potoo bird which might not have been as gaily decorated as many of the others but its quizzical expressions always made her smile and they always seemed so industrious. Goodness only knows what they were doing.

All the parakeets and toucans and horn bills would be disturbed whenever a gaggle of potoo birds turned up where they were resting. As the evenings came and went so the rarer birds had made an appearance. There had been harpy eagles looking down wondering at the antics of the Royal flycatchers who were in turn mesmerized by the dancing patterns of the blue Morpho butterflies flitting among the lower boughs that surrounded them.

Grace had been given a book with pictures of all the different animals that she might see on a visit through the Amazon River basin. So far she had already been able to identify quite a lot.

There had been a number of different types of monkeys that had crossed their paths already. Black spider monkeys had been the most common and every day large gangs of them could be seen leaping around in the gantry of the trees high ahead.

The howler monkeys could be heard all around with their raucous hooting and screeching which seemed only to frighten the smaller capuchin honkies and send them scurrying back into places of safety. Grace had been hoping to catch a glimpse of a golden tamarin but none had crossed their paths as yet.

Drinking at the water edge had been scores of families of capybara that looked like giant hairy hamsters and were largely ignored by the other animals. She had seen a couple of black giant otter lurking in the shadows quietly watching as the canoe with the Fyfe family serenely flowed on past them. That had been near where all those paradise tanager birds had been putting on a courtship display as if they had been waiting for the canoe to come gliding along.

It had all been such a magical adventure already, and as each day past so it seemed likely that the prospect of even more wondrous things lay ahead. There were some animals that Grace had never heard of before listed in her book, like the mata mata and the kinkajou and she was hoping to get a glimpse of those.

She did not expect to see a jaguar, that would have been asking too much, however there were still giant anteaters and side necked turtles to try and locate. All this without mentioning the prospect of seeing an anaconda or an eyelash viper or a green basilak lizard.

They had already seen plenty of iguanas and each and every one had sent a thrilling chill through her. Grace really loved seeing all these wild animals in their natural environment. It was so much nicer than seeing them in any zoo.

Even the small and tiny creatures were just marvelous to behold. She guessed that none of her school friends would have ever seen a peanut head bug or a seemingly endless trail of marauding bullet ants marching through the undergrowth. This really was proving to be the greatest adventure ever.

Suddenly, from a place of glorious tranquility catastrophe struck. That is the way of catastrophes.

Grace and Reggie had been very safely secured in the large canoe that had been slowly paddling through the sluggishly thick brown waters of the mighty Amazon River. The shoreline on either side was filled with the dark greens and menacing gloom of the forest.

It was raining. It always seemed to be raining out in the wildness. Even during those times when the sun was shining the tall trees prevented the rays of the sun from finding their way to where the canoe was traveling. Everything seemed very wet indeed. Even in those moments when the sunshine broke through you could not escape from the wetness.

Reggie was curled up asleep in Graces lap and she was mildly dozing off into intermittent sleep when the front of the canoe suddenly hit a large boulder that had been lurking hidden just below the surface of the river. The entire boat had instantly turned over and every one of the passengers had been instantly thrown into the endlessly flowing brown ooze.

Steve and Katie were thrown to the left of the boat into shallow waters closer to the riverbank. Grace was tossed through the air to the right into the faster flowing currents and in an instant found herself being dragged away into the middle of the river.

Grace was immediately sucked downwards and desperately struggled to get her head back above the surface. It was all a mad blur of panic and terror.

In the sudden madness Grace though that she could see her parents scrambling ashore and turning to call desperately to her. Her head went below the water again and then as if by magic this great pink blob came beside her and helped to take her struggling band flailing body back up to the surface.

She now had absolutely no idea what was happening. This large pink object seemed to be joined by others and she found herself being propelled across the width of the mighty brown river to the thick dirty mangrove roots of the opposite shore. Far to the right from where her parents had been stranded to the left.

Grace was able to grasp a branch and could now take in huge gulps of air. Below her feet could finally feel the relief of solid ground and she realized that she could pull herself ashore across the intricate patterns of roots that were climbing through the thick brown mud that engulfed them.

Grace was in a state of shock for herself. As the enormity of these events began to sink in Grace was suddenly aware that Reggie was not with her. She spun around frantically and was utter amazed to see that there were huge pink snouts pushing her bedraggled little puppy through the water straight towards her. It was a miracle.

Had Grace been able to look at her book of animals of the Amazon she would have discovered that she had been rescued from drowning by the now rare pink Amazon River dolphin. They have been known to help human stragglers before, but they are a very rare sight in modern times as their habitat has been severely disrupted by human activity.

The small pod of dolphins just swam off as if nothing had happened and left a little girl and a small puppy stranded in the mud on the side of a river in a place that could quite easily be described as "the middle of no-where".

Grace knew that she had to act swiftly now and try and force her way inwards to reach more solid land. She was able to scramble slowly through the heavy mud and little Reggie was managing to struggle in an exhausted way through the tangle of slimy wood just alongside her.

After a number of minutes that seemed like an entire lifetime Grace crashed over those brutal branches that were drooping over the river. At last she felt that the floor was secure and felt she had managed to actually have clambered her way to the safety of some sodden muddy land. To her great relief little Reggie had dragged himself along in the same way and was able to force his way through the brambles to where she lay breathless, scared and shivering with shock and the sudden coldness that enveloped her.

Across the murk she was able to see her parents on the far shore behind her. Stave and Katie were frantically waving and shouting but they really were far too far away to be able to hear what they were calling. The empty canoe was now far ahead in the distance being dragged by the flow of the river further and further away and was very soon out of sight altogether.

It was all so terribly peculiar. One minute they were just a happy little family slowly drifting down a river all very secure and safe. Then, just a few moments later everything had been turned Topsy-turvy. Her parents were stranded all the way over there and Grace and Reggie found themselves wet and cold and alone by the side of a huge river in one of the most remote places in the world.

The distance between Grace and her parents was really much too far for them to swim. Everyone knows that there are parts of that river where there a piranha fish that are dangerous, and that there are all kinds of other animals that need to be given the greatest possible respect.

The river was known for electric eels and no end of huge fish with big teeth. Swimming really was not an option. So both little groups needed to consider their new situation very carefully indeed.

Should they stay where they had found themselves and hope that someone would realize that they were missing and that a rescue party would be sent?

Perhaps they could try and head back down the river to attempt to reach the last village they had passed about twenty miles away? Or maybe they should seek to travel up the river to see if there was a village that was any nearer in that direction.

There was no point in even beginning to think that they should travel inland away from the river because the rain forest was far too thick to walk though and there was little chance of finding anyone to help in among that seemingly endless green wilderness.

Well Grace was a clever girl and had very quickly realized that the best option for her and Reggie was to stay exactly where they were and hope that help would arrive. On the distant shore it seemed that her parents had come to the same conclusion, and it was reassuring for her to see them waving to her. She could see that they were again shouting messages to her, but they were simply too far away for her to hear what they were saying.

Even if the rain forest had been perfectly quiet she would not have been able to hear them and, it is the way of rain forests that they are never quiet. There is always far too much going on there for anything remotely like silence to ever occur.

Grace had always been a very brave girl but this really was a very difficult situation that she found herself in and so hugely scary that she felt overwhelmed and she began to cry. Beside her little Reggie was trying to shake the water off himself and only managed to make her even wetter, as if that were possible. Then he snuggled against her and tried his best to cheer her up. Puppies are not always good at realizing how much danger they find themselves in.

Perhaps things might have been better if she were not quite so wet? Maybe she might have felt a little better if she had been a nit warmer? So this is how the adventure in the rain forest started for a bright and lovely eight year old girl who was stranded with her puppy many miles and miles from anywhere.

Chapter Three

SETTING UP CAMP

It takes a little while to come to terms with shocking events no matter what age you are. Your brain has to absorb all kinds of new information and try to adjust to all the different thoughts and emotions that come flooding in. At the same time there are a hundred different physical demands that need to be taken into consideration. People will always be stunned and dazed when they are unexpected lurched into a big muddy river, be it Amazon or any other waterway you could mention.

After a few minutes Grace realized that just sitting down in the mud and crying was not going to help her and that she should be starting to do something to make her situation better.

Her first thought was that it would be best if she could try and make some kind of shelter, just to try and keep the rain from constantly falling on her. Because it was cold it crossed her mind that it would also be good if she could start a fire, but both of these things were enormous tasks for a small girl to try and do all by herself.

Back in Britain Grace had been in the Brownies and had an idea that someone could start a fire if they rubbed two sticks together. Yet although she was surrounded by trees for hundreds and hundreds of miles in every direction it seemed like an impossible task. She would have needed dry twigs and there was nothing in the whole of the rain forest that was in any way dry at all.

On the positive front she knew that if she collected branches and stacked them together she could make some kind of rough shelter for herself. Hopefully this might form some kind of shape that would provide some relief from the constant rainfall and a little bit of protection from the wild elements.

As you can imagine this proved a lot more difficult than she had thought. Making a shelter is a hard-enough task in any circumstances and these were very trying matters altogether. It all seemed so much easier in the gentle woods of Britain, here in Brazil absolutely everything seemed to be designed to be at least five times more difficult for her.

All of the branches seemed to be attached to trees and there was no easy way of cutting them off. It was not as if she had been carrying a knife or a saw or an axe with her when she had been pitched into the muddy river. So she found a place where the trees and the foliage seemed to be thickest and tried to nestle a shape for herself and Reggie to rest. She was able to collect lots of leaves and twigs and tried her best to make a nest, but everything was just so sodden that it seemed hopeless.

Far away, on the other side of the river she could see her parents were scuttling around trying to do the same thing. It was really exhausting work and Grace was now on top of being very scared and frightened and cold and wet and miserable and lonely.

Poor young Grace started to feel very thirsty and hungry too. What on Earth was she going to do? All of the supplies were either still in the canoe floating off into the distance or else at the bottom of the River Amazon being nibbled by fish and never to be seen again.

It perhaps seems strange that she felt thirsty, just a couple of hours earlier she had been thrown in a river and had felt like she was drowning. At the same time, she was soaking wet and was scrabbling around in constant rain. However somehow that sort of water all seems very, very different from the type of clear drinking water that you can find in a bottle or coming out of a tap.

Grace looked around her to see if there was anything at all that she could use as a container to try and collect the rainwater that was falling all around her. She could not see anything at all that would help her and so she just sat on a branch with her mouth open trying to drink in the water that was dripping through the canopy of the huge trees around her and hoping that this water was clean enough to be able to drink safely.

Grace was clever enough to know that finding food was soon going to be a really big problem for her as she was going to wait to be rescued. However, she thought that she could start to think about that in the morning. In the rain forest the evenings are very short and it becomes night-tine very quickly, and she thought that her first priority would be to make sure that her overnight shelter was safe. She used the last rays of the sun to find more twigs and small branches and tried her best to pile them up before the blackness of night fell on her.

On the other side of the river she could see a small light flickering and that told her that her parents had managed to start a fire over there. That made her feel a bit more comfortable. It meant that any rescue party might be able to see smoke and realize where they were.

With the last moments of daytime, she waved frantically across to her desperately anxious parents to say goodnight and they waved beck in an equally frantic manner. What else could they possibly do? Grace settled down as best she could and snuggled up close to Reggie, who had stayed firmly close to her feet the whole time.

Grace had thought that the forest would very quiet and still when night-time fell. She very quickly came to realize that this was an extremely erroneous piece of thinking. As soon as the sky turned to complete darkness all manner of noises sprang up all around her. Grace had never heard any of those cries and hoots before, there were all manner of screams and endless creaking and hurried scutterings and rustling and it became a deafening cacophony.

Each and every new sound was more frightening than the last and soon Grace was a shivering wreck again, sitting in terror desperately waiting for the Sun to come back again. She was convinced that she would start to feel braver in the light. She was shivering with the coldness of the night and spent the hours waiting desperately for the warmth the morning sun would bring.

For some unknown reason the thought of a Jaffa cake popped into her mind. All her life she had taken things like having sweets and regular meals and her own bed to sleep in every night totally for granted. They were just always there, and now they were totally out of her life altogether. Just one little Jaffa cake would be so wonderful. But this was not a place where any cake or sweet treat would be coming her way.

She wondered what she could do to help Reggie. It was not as if there was going to be any bowl of water or dog food for him. Oh, it was all so worrying. Amid all the wild noises and the extreme anxiety Grace suddenly thought that perhaps that she would never fall asleep again. Yet, sometime between the disappearances of that indifferent sun and its return in the glorious dawn of the morrow a troubled slumber befell her tired and weary body so tightly curled up amid the rough pile of discarded leaves and twigs of the forest floor.

Chapter Four

HUNTERS

Grace woke up. Her makeshift bed of twigs and leaves had not been comfortable in any way. Bits of wood had been digging into her but she realised that none of the many insects had bitten her. When she stood up it was very clear that the forest was being kind to her. Who would have thought that a Brazilian rain forses5t would be friendly to s young Welsh girl? At her feet a small cuddly brown dog seemed very contented that his best friend had woken up and was ready for the next adventure that was going to come their way.

Grace was just so very happy that Reggie was with her and that he was safe, but she was also feeling very lonely indeed. She had imagined that she and her puppy had been quite alone all night out is the wild forest and jungle lands of the riverbank. Little did she realize that many thousands and thousands of eyes had been looking at the strangers from the trees and bushes and all the surrounds.

None of them were human eyes, but the land is filled with creatures of all types and sizes who are both hunters and hunted according to the wilds laws of Nature. There are insects and rodents there are birds and mammals, lizards and shakes. Flying above are bats and moths. Occasional monkeys and sloths. Voles and frogs are all looking for food and watching out to try and make sure that they do not become a dinner for something else. None of them had ever seen an eight-year-old British girl with a small brown puppy before and they presented new smells to consider and another possible thing to worry about.

Until now Reggie had been really very quiet, just shivering and pressing himself as close to Grace as he could. Suddenly he started barking and went scampering off into the undergrowth. Grace jumped up to make sure that he was safe. She need not have worried, Reggie came back with a small rodent in his mouth and seemed very happy with himself. He put the little animal down and it rushed off into the leaves with a lucky escape.

However, it was clear that Reggie was probably going to be able to look after himself whilst they were waiting for help to come. Grace looked out at the wide slow-moving muddy river hoping to see a canoe out in the water searching for her, but there was no boat in either direction.

Her parents were already moving about and they waved across to each other to reassure one another as best they could. She knew that her Mother and Father would be beside themselves with worry about her, so she tried to make her waving as cheerful as she could. Their fire was still alight and a thin trail of smoke was weaving a path up through the trees. Perhaps a search plane might be sent out for them she thought hopefully. She looked upwards but she could barely see the sky though the trees and certainly not any airplanes.

It was then that Grace caught her first site of a tarantula. There it was calmly sitting on a branch just by the pile of leaves that she had used as her bed last night. It was about eight inches long and was sitting perfectly still just staring at her in quiet contemplation. He seemed to be just sizing her up and was not aggressive or particularly scary. It was just big and, in comparison to other animals which are deemed to be rather more pleasing to the eye, seemingly quite ugly.

Grace had never been so close to any arachnid, never mind one that was bigger than her hand. She screamed and jumped backwards. However, the tarantula did not move but just calmly kept looking at her. Grace also kept looking at him, wondering if the spider would suddenly jump out at her. The longer she looked the more detail she was able to see. The legs were actually quite furry, the face was actually really quite interesting. This was not the way she had expected to start her day.

Behind her Reggie started barking. Grace turned to make sure that he was alright and when she turned back the tarantula had disappeared just as elusively as it had arrived. Now Grace was a clever girl, she knew better than to annoy or provoke any animal and that they were far more likely to be more scared of her than she would be of them. She felt quite pleased with herself that she had coped quite so well in this situation. She felt that a lot of her friends at school would not have managed this little confrontation as well as she had done.

Grace knew that the forest was full of different wild animals and that she would probably have lots of new encounters like this whilst she waited for help to come rescue her. It was actually quite thrilling to be so close to creatures who were not pets. but is was also quite scary.
Grace told Reggie that he must definitely not bother any tarantulas, but she was fairly certain that he did not understand her. Nine-month-old puppies do not listen to instructions from eight-year-old girls. Gracie told Reggie that she loved him very much and that he was the best puppy in all the world. He seemed happy to be given some attention. Grace knew that he must be very hungry and thirsty too.

All along the rough shoreline nearby to where they had scrambled ashore were lots of giant lily plants that had really wide leaves. Grace was able to pull a couple of these clear and was able to fashion them into bowl shapes so they could capture the rainwater and be suitable for both her and the little dog to drink from. This only took about half an hour and it seemed to Grace that she had achieved something very positive and it made her feel a little more confident.

She was so busy concentrating of completing this task that she did not notice that Reggie had gone off hunting and had returned to her side happily chewing on a frog. Well, it was not the sort of meal he usually had but it was better than nothing. She hoped that it would not make him ill, but Reggie was wagging his tail and seemed very pleased with himself.

Grace was wondering what she could eat. She hoped that there would be all sorts of wild fruits and berries that she might be able to eat but was also concerned that they might be poisonous and make her ill. Yet it seems that it is much harder to find fruits growing in the Amazon area than you might think.

Whilst she had been given a book telling her about the different animals she might encounter not quite so much attention had been provided in respect of the flora. There were thousands of different types of trees but none that she could readily identify.

It seemed to her that they all seemed to have very difficult names such as jacarand, filus and inga but she really could not remember many of them or identify what they looked like. She had seen the tall wimba trees reaching high over all the others all along their journey down the river but in among all the trees at ground level all the trunks looked much the same.

Then there were vines and occasional flowers like orchards and water lettuce and passion palms. What Grace was hoping to see were banana plants or coconut trees, but there were none around. Even a Brazil nut tree would have been helpful, but they were all seemingly elsewhere in the vastness of the tropical wetlands.

Grace did not want to move very far away from the space she was using as her camp and went a few yards in every direction scrambling through the branches and the undergrowth but she could not see any fruit trees at all. There was a bush that had some very hard dirty red berries on that was covered in ants and she did not want to risk eating those.

She wondered about trying to go fishing but she knew that she could not make a fire with all the wet wood and did not want to eat a raw fish. In fact, she thought that she was surrounded by all kinds of possible types of food but that she would not be able to cook any of them, It was clear that this was going to be a big problem for her.

The thoughts of Jaffa cakes came into her mind again. She thought to herself that it would be really wonderful if she could find herself a Jaffa-cake tree behind the next clump of bushes, but all that was there were more horrible bushes with thorns and little brown and black ants.

By the start of the afternoon Grace was feeling really hungry and knew that she had to try and eat something. Eventually she found a plant that had leaves that were quite soft and pulpy so she chewed on those. They tasted a bit like grass, but slightly bitter, and at least it made her feel like she was eating something.

Grace hoped that this plant would not make her ill, and it seemed like it was alright, just not a very nice taste and not very substantial. Grace vowed to herself that she would never moan about any meal she ate ever again.

In the meantime, Reggie appeared to be quite adept in catching those little frogs and he seemed to be settling into his new living situation quite well. Along the river there were all kinds of different birds sitting in the trees and splashing into the water. Sometimes there were flocks of brightly coloured birds higher in the canopy that flashed into view for just a moment.

Every couple of hours Grace would wave across to her parents to let them know that she was safe and they would wave back and try to make signs with their arms, but Grace could not make out what message they were trying to tell her. Of course, all their mobile phones had not survived the fall into the river.

It was only a few days ago that Grace had flown from her home in Britain all the way across the ocean to get to Brazil. Her parents had won a competition managed by Adventure Magazine with the first prize of an exciting family holiday of a canoe trek through the Amazon rain forest.

Everyone had been so excited and looking forward to this opportunity of a lifetime. Less than a fortnight before jetting off across the Atlantic Ocean Grace had been at home watching television as normal, having lunch as usual, chatting to her friends from school and just having as ordinary a life as any other girl might, and now her she was sleeping in a forest with her small brown puppy and not living like any other girl in all the world.

At a time she guessed would have been around five o'clock in the evening the tarantula made another appearance on the same branch. Grace was not sure what is was that tarantulas actually eat. Was it plants or other little animals? It all made her think of Jaffa cakes again and so she deliberately made herself think of something else altogether.

She thought that it might be helpful if she were to make a large sign of some kind so that if a boat were to come down the river or an airplane be flying over then they could see that someone was staying by the side of the river and come along to see what was going on. It sounded like a good idea but Grace could not think of what she could use that would attract attention in that way. Everything was just so much harder to do here than she thought it would be.

In the distance there was a new sound, it was a strange sort of whooping and high pitch shouting. Grace guessed that it would be monkeys of some kind, although she had never heard that noise in her life before so it was really just a guess. Reggie didn't seem to like these new sounds too much and started barking into the trees, but that did not stop the sounds echoing around.

Suddenly it all when quiet again as the evening sky once more turned into night and that wild excitement started up once more and the whole of the rain forest was filled with the calls of wild things lurching though the encroaching black stillness that crawled across the Earth.

Chapter Five

HIDDEN DANGERS

Reggie was barking wildly. He was jumping up and down and snarling in a way that Grace had never seen before. As far as she could tell there was nothing there. The whole of the forest was just complete blackness. On the other side of the river was a small twinkle where her parent's fire was still alight but everything else was as if the whole planet had been buried in soot. Grace patter her pet and tried to calm him but little Reggie was beside himself with excitement. It was clear that something had spooked him but goodness only knows what it might have been.

With the coming of the morning light Grace discovered who the overnight visitor was. In the wet muddy floor by the river were the tale0tell signs of a big cat. Grace had been told that sometimes Pumas will come to the river to drink and that is what must have happened.

Well, this was a sinister turn of events. Grace had been so very terrified when first she fell into the river and somehow splashed her way to the shoreline. Then the magnitude of the severity of the dilemma she found herself in was overwhelming. Gradually she had been slowly coming to terms with her predicament and now this new peril emerging threw her back into a state of panic.

How dangerous is a prowling jaguar to a young girl alone in a forest? Grace reckoned that was just about as dangerous a situation as there could possibly be. Perhaps Reggie barking had been enough to cause the stealthy visitor to turn around and return to its light-less lair? Just last week she had been bouncing around on the trampoline in her garden without a care in the world. Now she is faced with the reality of being stalked by a huge cat with a known appetite for isolated human children.

Whilst Grace really did not know too much about the dietary preferences of the jaguar she did know that they had huge teeth that can rip their prey apart and strong paws and claws that can rip those things that they hunt. There are many things in life that you might not wish to be and one of those things almost certainly something that a jaguar might want to have for its dinner.

It was then Grace caught site of a different set of footprints in the mud. These were quite different in shape quite long and flat with a deep hook in the end. Between these prints was a deep trail as if something had been dragged along. It was clear that these had been left by a visiting alligator or cayman.

This was just another thing to worry about. Grace wondered if it might be better if she tried to build herself a little shelter in the branches of a tree so that she and Reggie could sleep away from the ground. It would require a lot of work and she was starting to feel quite fatigued because she had only been eating those pulpy leaves and they were not seeming to be a very good source of energy for her.

As she was considering this possibility the tarantula made a morning appearance again and that made her wonder again if sleeping in a tree would be any safer than sleeping on the ground. There were just so many things to worry about.

All her cloths were now filthy dirty from all the grime and mud from the moment she had fallen into the river and they were sticky and cold and wet and ripped in places. Since coming ashore, she had been constantly wet and uncomfortable so she was feeling pretty wretched and frightened and quite sorry for herself. But it was a terrible situation to be in and probably everyone in the world would have felt the same way.

Grace tried to cheer herself up by waving to her parents and throwing small twigs for Reggie to fetch. It has to be said that little brown puppies are very good at helping to cheer people up. Grace was very lucky to have been born with a very happy disposition and she was able to face hardship in a very positive way. At home her family would call her "a happy little sausage" as a term of affection because she was one of those girls who was able to make everyone around them happy. It was just a gift that she was born with.

Grace went off to pick a few more of those green pulpy leaves for lunch and looked around again to see if there was anything else around that might be a bit tastier. When she came back she saw that the tarantula had been joined by another large spider on the branch near to where she had been sleeping. The more she looked at them the more interesting she thought they were. In turn, they seem fascinated by her and their eyes followed her every movement intently. It felt a little unnerving. She felt that these two spiders were incredibly wise but she had no idea why she felt this way.

"When we get rescued I will try and find out a bit more about all the spiders in the rain-forest", she said to Reggie. Of course, Grace was a very optometric little girl and had always believed that she would be somehow be saved from the difficult situation they found themselves in.

Chapter Six

CALLERS

Grace heard a switching sound and caught the signs of some movement from the corner of her eye. She was suddenly completely shocked.

From out of the scruffy thorny bushes poked the head of an old man. Well that was just the last thing that she had expected. He was not alone, behind him were a small group of other old men who were creeping though the thick mass of branches, vines, bushes and undergrowth that encircled her little encampment area.

One of the most noticeable about them is that none of them were wearing very much in the way of clothing. They were all bare from the waist upwards with their brown skins covered in strange black and red tattoos and markings. All were wearing just an identical dark green coloured knee length skirt, no shoes and so were travelling barefoot through that difficult jungle-like terrain. Perhaps it was a uniform because they all looked very similar to one another?

To the eyes of a young British girl who had never been abroad before Grace was fully accustomed to everyone that she met to be fully attired so to see a small gaggle of older men wearing just strips of clothing around their waist was unexpected.

They seemed to be pleased to have come across her and were very excited to see little Reggie. It was as if they had never seen a girl or a puppy before and they chatted very quietly and excitedly among themselves. For his part Reggie was grinning with that huge smile he used when he was at his happiest and he appeared to be very pleased to meet these new people after those days of isolation. To him they might not be dogs, but they seemed like the next best thing.

Grace was very relieved indeed to see them. She thought that this must be a search party that had been sent out to find her.

She stretched out her had to shake their hands and say hello, but these men did not seem to understand that gesture. She gestured for them to follow her and she took them the few yards to the edge of the river and waved across to her parents.

Grace was very keen to let her folks know that they had been round and help was at hand. Grace waved wildly across the water and her parents saw her and waved wildly back. Grace pointed to the men who were standing around her,

The men did not wave back but seemed very excited in seeing two other people on the other side of the river standing beside a small fire with smoke going up into the trees.

Grace was really excited, she had assumed that the men had traveled down the river by canoe and would now simply paddle her across the wide river to where her parents were and then carry them all on to the next village and then onto safety. It did not occur to her that these men might not have a boat.

The old men were all very short and skinny. Their peculiar tattoo designs seemed more like maps than pictures of animals or anything like that. She then noticed that none of the men had any teeth. They were mainly quite bald and moved around very slowly and deliberately, talking in a strange language with lots of small clicks and gentle whistles. They seemed friendly. Grace was suddenly very aware that she was incredibly dirty and that her long hair had not been brushed for days and was quite filthy.

The men looked around the little camp she had made and clicked and whistled gently to each other. Reggie started barking at them so Grace patted him and calmed him down and was smiling to the men. Quite frankly, she had never been so happy to see anyone in all of her short life.

She pointed to herself and said "My name is Grace" but they did not seem to understand and just clicked away slowly, looking around all the time. Suddenly one of the men suddenly pounced and grabbed the two tarantulas that were sitting on the branch and seemed to crush them with his bare hands. He then pulled a leaf from the little tree and wrapped the two huge crumpled spiders in this leaf and folded them away in his waistband.

The men then started to wander away from the camp into the bushes and indicated that Grace and Reggie should go with them. She gave a frantic goodbye wave to her parents and set off into the forest. Of course, she was thinking that their canoe would be moored nearby. It seems Grace was just a bit too optimistic about this rescue. These six toothless tattooed old men did not have a canoe at all!

Chapter Seven

THE SONG OF THE TREES

In comparison to those who live in Brazil the people from Britain really do not know very much about trees. At one time before the ice age called to chase all the humans away to the warmer climes of Europe the whole of the land now called the United Kingdom was covered by a great and ancient forest.

It was a lively sort of place. There were elk and red panda and beavers playing in the woods all manner of birds and wolves lived in harmony with the land. The trees were content and nature prospered. Yet time is cruel and as it passed on a journey of its own the sheet ice and glaciers were banished to the North and mankind returned to these sacred isles.

With these more so-called "advanced" men and women came fire and iron and the axe and the saw. So it was that the trees were felled and the forests became a vast empty moorland and the hills were stripped bare. The animals were gone and those mighty ones that watch these things were moved to tears.

It seemed that Mankind lost the understanding of the ways of trees. Humans no longer seemed to not realize that all living things communicate in manners beyond the comprehension of the minds of men. Trees cam inform each other of moving waters and the flight of insects and plights and blights, Plants will inform insects who will tell others in secret ways of the changes for good and ill that befall the soil. They use chemicals detected in the wind and changes in hue.

Understanding these sacred matters is seen as the ways of witches and sages and the wisdom of ancient lore. These new humans in their endless greed and folly and misplaced superiority have destroyed that which suckled them and brought them joy.

Perhaps this is the fate that destiny has cast us and there is a danger that things have gone too far. Yet there is hope.

There are voices clambering to be heard that are loudly exclaiming that humans have to take account of their environment. There are calls across the whole globe for a greater awareness of these issues and for humans to change the way they have been spoiling to wonderful resources of the planet they are living on.

Nowadays the young people of the world are starting to discover all these things and can begin to work together to make a better world for themselves and all the amazing creatures we share this Earth with.

In the wild places there are still remnants of the ancient tribes who hold faith with the woods and understand the winds and sod. Just pockets of souls who whisper and whistle to those ancient sounds that give meaning to stone and branch and the travels of the air we share.

So it was that deep in the Amazon, for from the destruction of steel and coal the six humble shaman of ages past gathered when the river and the trees informed them of a lost child saved from drowning.

She had been protected by the forest and guarded by a jaguar, protected by the land, fed by the pulpy mass of life saving protein grass and honored by the emperors of all spiders. With a trusty companion yapping love and comfort the forest sustained her long enough for the shaman to call and bring her out of peril.

Humans will never even start to understand the mighty river and the trees that give oxygen and life to all the planet. With their whispers and their wisdom, they sing with the trees the song of life that sustains us all,
"So it is the tree and the wind.
So it is the soil and all breath.
Let us love that which we know is true
Let us treasure and rejoice in the gift we share."

The six toothless men came from a time before the hills had risen from the primal sea. They came before time was fully formed and played its wicked tricks on the hearts of angels. Just these six endangered souls left to help confront that ceaseless tide of greed that is relentlessly choking the arteries of our world.

So it was these six wise and sacred men took Grace away from the river and the dangers of the night and made their way though the mighty trees and the holy lands past the highways of the secret wisdom. Young Grace was being taken into the very heart of the rain forest. Anywhere else at any other time this would almost certainly be a very bad thing to do. However, there was a deeper magic at play here and it just seemed exactly the right thing to do.

The Amazon is home to a trillion secrets. Some we know about such as the unfathomable lines the Nazca peoples were mistakenly said to have scraped away and those immense hooded stone Olmec heads that shouted across the mountains.

The way of the unwritten winds and the gentle caress of the hidden seas had cast spells all around those mighty trees. Inside the woods and jungles were all the inexplicable and unimagined hidden hexes that forged the wondrous designs that humans have glibly called "nature".

The party halted on occasion to eat the fruits of some strange little bushes. The berries looked and felt like figs but tasted more like a nutty avocado. Grace was very pleased to have a change from that other plant she had been   eating.

Then they came across a banana tree and Grace was finally able to eat enough to stop her feeling hungry. In the meantime, Reggie had been regularly catching small animals from the depths of the bushes they passed and it seemed like he also was being blessed by the rain forest too.

Eventually the six toothless man arrived with a very scruffy eight-year-old British girl in in muddy torn dress who sported long unkempt and wild hair at the entrance of a cave. She did not know it but this place was the holy and sacred Temple of the Golden Skull.

Alongside her was a nine-month-old puppy called Reggie. Neither of them had any idea that they had been rescued from the darkness and brought to this place for a mighty purpose. For that which is written that the ways of the holy are beyond all comprehension of those trapped in temporal guises.

Who are we to question the ways of those immaculate forces we simply cannot possibly know?

Chapter Eight

THE HOLY TEMPLE

Grace was really very glad indeed when the small party of rescuing old men finally stopped at the entrance of a small cave hidden in the depths of the rain forest. Once she was inside the cave Grace started to feel a little bit warmer for the first time in days. Also, she realized that she was not as wet. People do not seem understand that rain-forests are very wet places – there is a clue in the name.

She felt that she could sit down comfortably for the first time and, at long last, she was given a hard leaf layered with food that she could eat properly and a warm drink. It seems quite a small pleasure but after all those hours of fear and worry by the river this place seemed like heaven.

As it happens it was not a particularly big cave that she found herself sheltering in yet it had four distinct passages leading off in different directions. Two seemed to have lights further along and a couple whispered quiet sounds that seemed to somehow express joy. It was a strange place and Grace had never been anywhere quite like it before.

The strange toothless men fussed around her with their quiet clicks and whispers and little whistles and they somehow sounded to her like the wind blowing across a barley field and the sounds of waves crashing on a shore. Grace was not quite sure how to explain it but she felt very safe and at peace.

After the really horrible few days she had experienced it was a relief just to be able to be calm. Without realizing it she dropped off to sleep and beside her little Reggie was also entering a state of deepest slumber.

The glorious hands of destiny were weaving a spell around Grace and Reggie and the six wise men gave praise to whatever it might be that created us all for the honour of being a small part of the priceless duty that was due to take place.

Goodness only knows how long it was that the girl and her small russet brown dog resided in their state of sleeping bliss. It was long enough for them to feel both relieved and refreshed and curious about what the next stage of their journey might be,

On waking it appeared that three of the old men had left the cave and the three who remained were sitting at points near to main entrance and making those strange noises that just seemed to make them appear in complete unity with the simplicity of the walls that encircled them.

Grace was not quite sure how to explain it, but she was experiencing a sense of "holiness" that was entirely new to her. There was certainly nothing like this place anywhere over in Brain or, if there was, she had never been told about it.

Grace was concerned about being separated from her parents. When she had been stranded at the edge of the river it had been comforting to know that she could wave to Steve and Katie and that they would know that she was safe. Now that they were distanced not just by a river but also many miles of uncharted forest it was vexatious. Grace had expected that they would have all been reunited by now, instead of which they were even further apart than what they had been yesterday.

However, Grace was a very sensible girl. She realized that she had been incredibly lucky to have been rescued from her ramshackle makeshift little shelter and was very grateful to have had been provided with sustenance and refreshment.

The six old men had offered her some peculiar new clothes to wear. Well, it was actually two lengths of the same dark green cloth that they were using. Grace fashioned herself a shirt and a sari type top which seemed to be just ideal for the humidity of the forest. It was difficult to describe quite how she looked but it was perhaps something like a two-piece toga. Anyway, it was nice to be able to feel so much dryer and cleaner.

After she was fed and fully refreshed the most senior of the toothless men took Grace into the first of the tunnels inside the cave. After a short distance she found herself in a small chamber filled with light.

In the middle of this space was a large stone that seemed to be an alter and resting on this surface was an inscribed and highly illustrated document. It had a script that seemed to change design as she looked at it. After several changes the script turned to English and she was able to read the following instructions.
"Step forward Child of light to complete your glorious task.
You have been chosen to unchain the forsaken soul
You will give breath to that most holy re-awakening
Comest thou dutiful child to dutiful to your appointed hour
Bindings will be cut and blindness cast asunder.
Condors will soar free again above this despoiled land.
Blessed are thee, Child of hope."

Well Grace was an eight-year-old girl and all this sounded pretty serious to her. Basically, all she wanted to happen was to be back home with Steve and Katie and jumping on her trampoline and eating Jaffa-cakes.

Grace was not too sure that she wanted all the responsibility of being a "Child of hope". It really did sound like a very grown up thing to be and Grace actually really liked just being an eight-year-old girl and not having to worry too much about grown up things until the moment that she really had to. Being a girl should be fun, right?

Still the old man seemed very keen for her to go with him into the next tunnel. He beckoned her to follow him and she obliged. This was an even shorter passageway and took them into a chamber that was dark but filled with many layered gentle sounds.

At first it was hard to differentiate between all the different noises but after a couple of minutes she was able to isolate the ripple of water in a stream, then of the wafting wind on a stormy night, then low birdsong across a distant meadow, then children in a playground and the laughter of gathered friends: moment by moment there was new clarity as a choir and a call to prayer and wind chimes and badgers burrowing, each new sound forming wonderful pictures in her mind. What a glorious place this was.

The next passage was a room full of statues of people who seemed broken in spirit and yet somehow residing in peace, It was a room full of contraction it was a space where truth and heresy held hands and danced in union.

Grace felt that she did not understand this room, yet, at the very end there was a wooden statue of a young girl dressed in a dark green robe and by her side was a small dog that looked remarkably like Reggie. Grace did not feel particularly at ease in seeing this and was pleased to be led away into the forth tunnel.

This final entrance took them to a slightly longer path to walk which had a number of narrow twists along the way. Finally, they arrived in a small anti camber and all that was in this room was a plinth in the farthest corner and on display way a perfectly formed skill made entirely from amber.

All around, scattered on the floor were unformed pebbles that appeared to be made of amber too. As she approached the skull seemed to be resonating a gentle whirring noise. This old man bowed before this skull and appeared to hold it in the highest possible reverence.

Everything that she was seeing was entirely new to Grace, all these strange things and amazing experiences were really quite overwhelming. However, the next thing that happened was just so unexpected and inexplicable that she felt that it would be impossible to ever properly describe what happened next.

The old man reached into his waist band and removed the packed leaf that contained the two seemingly dead tarantulas that he had captured. He then proceeded to place one of the crumpled spiders into each of the vacant eye sockets on the face of the amber skull. It was as if she were watching some ritual that resonated from the deepest recess of human history.

The venerable artifact seemed to have an inner golden glow of great majesty. To her amazement both of the spiders very slowly started to unfold themselves and both suddenly sprang back into life and seemed just as bright and alert as they had done before they had been so brutally crushed the day before.

Grace had no idea what was the meaning of this unbelievable arachnid resurrection that she was witnessing. However, the old man seemed very relieved by this turn of events and gave her a toothless smile to suggest that something quite wonderful had occurred, as indeed it had.

It was some time later that Grace learned more of the sacred ways of the forest and the strange hierarchy that existed among the creatures who were seeking to survive the onslaught of human greed. She learned that it was the jaguar, the sea eagle and the tarantula who were the key keepers of the ancient lore and secret rites of ancient wisdoms.

These were the blessed animals that had been chosen and they had been trusted to follow a path of solitude in order to bring about the eventual healing of the wounds inflicted to the greater cosmos by those who had introduced the constructs of cruelty that has blighted the earth for so many eons now.

All Grace knew was that she was very pleased that the two tarantulas seemed to be happy and safe again. After her original feelings of fear in seeing them she had very quickly come to realize that they were actually very special creatures indeed.

Sometimes it seems there is a wisdom in children that simply cannot be explained to adult humans who seem to thrash about in ignorance and darkness when such matters are placed before them.

The ancient elder then led Grace back into the small chamber where the other two old men were waiting and little Reggie was wagging his tail happily. It all seemed so entirely dream-like that Grace could hardly believe what was happening to her. This is just the strangest and most wonderful place in the world she was thinking. No-one knows what Reggie was thinking but he really seemed very content with life and was seemingly loving every moment.

Then there was the moment of boundless joy. The three missing toothless men suddenly walked through the entrance and behind them came a very grubby, exhausted and relieved pair of parents.

Steve and Katie rushed to hug their daughter and it seemed that the hug was just the best and most wonderful hug there had ever been in all the world.

Chapter Nine

REUNION

Katie and Steve gushed that they had been incredibly worried watching from the other side of the river. They said they felt quite helpless as they saw their beloved daughter disappear into the darkness of the trees with those six strangers.

From where they were looking it was impossible to know if these men had good or bad intent and the terrible situation they were experiencing had suddenly become even worse. They had no way of knowing if Grace was safe and it was just a huge wrench to their hearts not to be able to even wave to help reassure her.

That night was by far the longest and most difficult they had ever experienced. Yet in the morning there were three old men in green skirts slowly walking through the endless tangle of trees that imprisoned them and they made friendly gestures to follow them. Steve and Katie were, of course concerned, who wouldn't be.

It was quite clear that these strangers did not like the fire that had so painstaking been set up and maintained by Steve. They made a great fuss in stamping it out with their bare feet. That made no sense, why did these people not like fire? Why did they not wear shoes?

However, Katie said that this would be a question for another time because they had been waiting for days in the vague hope that someone might come to rescue them and then these odd trio turned up and seemed to be wanting to help. It seemed as if the old men knew that the family were lost, but how could that possibly be?

Katie said that she too had thoughts that they would have a canoe nearby but that proved not to be the case. To Katie and Steve all of the rain forest looked much the same and one clump of trees was very much like the last. It was clear that these old men had a very different perspective and it appeared that they knew every single hidden pathway and passage through the wild undergrowth.

Not only did they know the layout of the land and the trees but they had a knowledge of all the secret passages that lay below the surface of the land. All across the world there are layers and layers of caves and passages that run beneath rivers and mountains and oceans.

Places that are so secret and holy they are beyond the realms of simple knowledge. These ancient men were able to lead Steve and Katie through the blackness of the subterranean highways and quite speedily to the little cave that was later know to them as the Temple of the Gold Amber Skull.

Katie and Steve had been quite simply starving, despite having a fire, neither of them had the bush craft to be able to actually catch any of the animals that had surrounded them. When it comes to the basics of nature it seems that humans might not be superior after all. So they ate the unusual beans, berries and fruits that were being offered to them with delight and relish.

Nourishment was a priority and taste had become an insignificant and irrelevant factor. It is funny on reflection to consider how priorities can change in an instant. What was important last week it seemed was now actually not of any value what-so-ever.

So it was that Grace and Reggie were happily reunited in a small cave somewhere in the beating heart of the rain-forest. They were utterly and comprehensively lost and no-one knew where they were or even that they were missing. Yet they were all as happy as they had ever been in all their lives. The little band of hapless travelers were just laughing and hugging and kissing each other in perfect happiness somewhere in a small dark hole in a place that had no name itself lost in the limitless wildness of the secret world.

Inside the cave this strange little group were gathered. In a nearby passage the Emperor and Empress of the Amazon tarantulas were starting to twitch their hairy legs. They were both trying to come to terms with the sudden turn of events that had befallen them. One minute they were on a branch looking at a lost girl by the river's edge in the next instant it seemed they were curled up in an eye socket of an amber skull. It is just not what they had been anticipating.

Unknown to the Fyfe family a lithesome jaguar was padding a way through the undergrowth to reach the place an appointment had been made from the dawn of time to undertake his part in a sacred ritual of renewal. Much further away a sea eagle was soaring high on warm winds ready to embark on the journey that had been selected for her from before the birth of history.

Looking down from on high for any unexpected interruptions. Nothing should disrupt the master plan of those most holy from whom all breath has been drawn that was proposed at the moment of the first dawn. There are deep mysteries out there that hold even deeper secrets within them. The universe does not spin by mere chance you know.

For this moment Grace and her parents and their little puppy were alive and had survived the first part of their ordeal. They did not know it at this particular moment of restoration but in the morning they were duet to set off of the next phase of their allocated pathway. They would need all the rest and recuperation time possible to regain their strength. Humans might not know much but they all seem to agree on this: the pathway to destiny is never going to be easy.

So it was that with the coming of the sun high above the trees outside the six whispering elders encouraged the little family to leave the small cave behind. It was clear that they were going to be moving on. Perhaps the old men would help them to get to a village where they could send out a message to let people know that they were missing but that they were safe?

Maybe, there would be a place where they could get a change of clothes and some food and someone to talk to who would speak English? Maybe they would be taken to a place where there was a canoe, or a boat or a plane? Grace was hoping that they might get to a place where there were Jaffa-cakes. However, the place that they were starting to journey towards had none of these things.

The pathway through the wild undergrowth and the secret paths under the hills was taking them slowly and securely to a place that was so remote and so secret that the only ones who knew about it were the people who lived there, the six wise elders and the animals of the rain forest who could never tell of its existence. This place was at the center of the heart of the Amazon.

In fact the place was so very well hidden that it did not have a name. The small tribe of people who lived there also did not have a name. Each of the dwellers of the secret place did not even have names of their own. Imagine living a life where no-one even had a name of their own. Well, humans have come to expect all manner of different things, but to most creatures having a name is a great privilege and most creatures never even have the possibility of getting a name of their own. Reggie could count himself very lucky in this respect.

As it happens when Graces' little puppy was born he had two brothers and three sisters in his litter and it had been expected that he would be known as "Chocky" because he was the darkest of all six puppies.

However, it was Grace that decided he should be known forever more as Reggie, somehow it just seemed to fit the way his broad chest and his wide smile presented themselves to the world. Reggie really liked the name he was given. So that seems to have worked out well for everyone.

Grace was pleased with her name. Katie was happy too. Steve was not that bothered but was glad that he had not been called Malcolm or Nigel which had been other possibilities mooted around the family at the time of his birth. Yes, there are a lot worse names in the world that people have to live with. The six ancient men and the tarantulas and the jaguar and the sea eagle have always been nameless.

It was our small desperate band of wayward travelers were making their way to the most secret lands where the hidden children of the founders thrive in isolation and solitude wrapped only in truth and free from the malice and cruelty that has corrupted our planet. Grace and Katie and Steve and Reggie were walking the untried paths to a place of innocence and wonderment.

It seemed an endless trudge because there was no sign to say where they were going or any notification that they had arrived. As is the way with these things, at one moment they were not there and the next minute they found themselves slap bang right in the center of a place that has always been and will forever remain unknown.

So what was it like? Well there were people and they were quiet and respectful. Like the elders they had only a strip of cloth around their waist for clothing. Their skin was dark and their hair was dark. They all had deep brown eyes that seemed both wise and shy at the same time. They did not smile but seemed content and extraordinarily serious.

There were shelters but they were not huts nor buildings of any conventional type they just seemed to be branches that had been roughly thrown together with no discernible pattern and yet not entirely in a random way either. There was a design, but it was not immediately obvious what that might be.

The only exception to this was a little construction located somewhere in the center of this bundle of strangeness. There was a small construction that seemed to be some kind of open prison made of rough branches. Inside this structure sat in complete isolation a small child. He looked as if he were about eight years old and somehow, he seemed quite different to all the other people of the settlement, because he had no face at all. Where a face should have been was simply a mass of deep wrinkles.

Grace was instantly filled with puzzlement. It appeared as if the entire area had been blighted by some melancholy and somehow this young boy was at the heart of whatever it was that was going on. Whilst the nameless people wandered around doing whatever it was they were trying to do it seemed obvious that they were all completely ignoring his little faceless boy.

Well Reggie was not used to this kind of behavior and was young enough to be indifferent to the subtleties of his surroundings. What he saw was a new little friend that he could play and so he went bounding up in his usual happy way with his broad smile and his bravest puppy strut and tried to get the youngster to play with him.

Grace too could sense that this little boy was essentially quite a nice little chap and went over to say hello too. She had not actually seen any other children since she had left on the plane from Britain a week ago and Grace was always happy to play with anyone else who was friendly too. We know she was a joyful sort of child and that is just the way that she had always been.

Now we know that Grace had been brought up nicely and had good manners and was kind. She had also been taught about the importance of recognizing difference and celebrating the fact that every single human being an animal is entirely different. To humans all ants look the same but to an ant all ants are very different. To an ant all humans look the same. So even though she was just eight years old Grace was very aware that these were important issues.

She knew that some people are scared or suspicious of people who are different to themselves and sometimes this can lead to nastiness and bullying and can be very negative. Grace was always very aware of that trap and would always seek to be kind and friendly to others. It was just the way she was. It was probably why she was the one who had been chosen from all of the people who had ever lived to undertake this particular mission.

It seemed that the little boy with no face did not understand what was happening. Perhaps no-one had ever tried to be friends with him before. After all, being born without a face does make someone a bit different from everyone else who does. It seemed as if the little boy did not know how to play at all.

Reggie was puzzled too. He had never come across a child who did not want his to chase after sticks that they threw away. He had never come across a child who did not want to stroke his head or would laugh when he rolled on his back to show them his tummy. Reggie knew that he was a really good puppy who knew how to make every child happy and it was most peculiar that this little boy did not seem to want to play with him.

Back in her home area Grace had lots of friends. People would say that she was lucky to have quite to many pals to play with, but, for those who understand such things it really was not anything to do with luck at all. What is was to do with was her spirit, it was the way that Gracie was that made her popular with the other children.

They knew that she was kind and that she was funny. She would share her secrets with them and would always keep her promises. She would share her sweets and listen to what other people had to say. Most of all Grace would share her gift of laughter, she had a lovely little giggle and the sweetest pretty smile. That is just the way that Grace was and it was really a very nice way to be altogether.

So just because this little boy did not know how to be friends with her was not the sort of thing that was going to put her off. If anything, it made her even more determined to try and make friends with him. So even though he did not speak the same language that she did, or that his expressionless face could not tell her what he was thinking about what she was saying Grace happily sat down beside the branches that roughly encircled him and chatted away merrily.

She told him all about how her parents had won a competition. She informed him about the exciting flight over the ocean as they flew in a huge airplane from Britain to Brazil and about the journey to the rain-forest where they picked up the canoe.

Grace jabbered away contentedly informing him about how the canoe had overturned and how horrible it had been being thrown into a muddy cold river and how scared that she had been. All about the panic of trying to scramble to safety and the worry of being separated from her parents and how wonderful it was that Reggie had not been washed away.

Then she continued to chatter on about how she had survived in the cold and wet and dangerous rain forest and all the different sounds that had scared her. Grace informed him of how hungry she had been and told him about the different animals she had seen and the ones she had imagined had been looking at her.

The boy sat still and it was not clear if he actually understood anything at all. From his perspective it had been a normal sort of day just like every other when all the people who had no name totally ignored him and then from nowhere this very strange young girl thing turned up with an unusual panting animal with big teeth and were making a strange fuss all around him.

Now for the faceless young boy nothing very much had ever happened, Day after day, week after week, year after year nothing had ever happened. He just sat in his allocated space and every moment was much the same as the previous one. Now, from absolutely nowhere an odd new girl had arrived and was just chuntering away merrily on the other side of his branches.

At the same time this crazed panting little, brown animal was wagging his rear wildly and grinning at him in an insane kind of way. It was all a bit overwhelming.

The little boy had never made a sound before. The others of the settlement had always assumed that he was both deaf and dumb. He had no features on his face and no-one had ever really seen if he had a mouth or eyes or ears because the whole of his face was just a mass of wrinkles that seems not to follow any design that could be described as a face.

So suddenly for the very first time in his life thy young boy made a noise. It would be difficult to explain just what sort of a noise it was, it was a sort of strangulated loud bleating sound. Just the very oddest sort of sound a young boy could make actually.

The effect of this was quite electrifying. It was if a magic wand had been cast over the settlement. For the past eight years all the nameless people had known only silence form this wrinkled little boy and now here he was able to bleat loudly in the face of these new strange creatures who had wandered into their living space. It was as big a shock as the whole community had ever experienced.

For the first time ever, the people with no names who were busy doing other things suddenly looked at the boy in the cage with new eyes. In an instant he had turned from the faceless silent boy who had no purpose to becoming the faceless young boy with the secret ability to bleat.

It was amazing. If you cannot understand how wonderfully amazing it was then image that you are going to visit your favourite Aunt and she has always had the same standard two arms that everyone else has. Then you call around to her house unexpectedly one Sunday afternoon and she answers the door and you discover that she actually has five arms but that she has always kept three arms a secret from you. That is how big a surprise it was to all the others who resided in the place where there were no names.

Chapter Ten

BIG SECRETS

So far this story has tried to tell you about a lovely young girl called Grace who found herself stranded deep in the Amazon rain-forest with her small brown puppy. Already it has been a pretty big adventure and she has had to face quite a lot of difficult situations. Now we have come to a place in the story where things become a little bit more difficult to understand.

Now this is not your fault. The whole of the universe is made up of all kinds of mysteries that nothing and no-one can ever understand. There are very deep mysteries all around the edge of all the known and unknown universes. Here are just a few examples. Where does time come from and where does it go when you are finished with it?

Who invented shadows and where do they go? Where do echoes stay hidden until they are called for. Why is coal black? Who made gravity? In fact, the whole of all our lives are simply full of both difficult and simple situations and questions that we will never really know the answer to. The trouble is, that humans have been designed to think that they do know the answers. It is just the way the human mind works.

Now animals do not pretend to know why water is wet or why the sun is hot, they just troll along quite happily not bothering too much about things that don't really bother them. Humans, on the other hand, are not like that at all. Humans have to meddle in all sorts of things that are none of their business and, because of this, humans are sometimes entirely to blame for messing things up.

Now if you were to ask all of the animals living in the Amazon rain forest what was the most annoying thing they have come across they would nearly all say the same answer – humans! Of course, not every human, but some men and women (mostly men) had started to do some things that were really very damaging indeed to the rain forest and the animals there have noticed this and it has made them very sad indeed.

There are all manner of very clever people who will talk with great expertise on "the laws of nature". Well in recent years scientist and researchers have conducted all sort of experiments and observations to try and explain the world we live in. They are hoping to discover the truth behind "the way things are". That is a pretty big task.

Why do birds instinctively know where to fly to or uninstructed fish find their way across oceans without decent maps? How do animals know weeks in advance of changes in the weather or when a volcano might erupt? Oh yes, there are no end of things to try and understand. Sometimes these experts will get it right and sometimes they will get it wrong. Everyone else has to plod along trying to work out which is which.

Now below all these very obvious sorts of actions and behaviours there are millions and millions of deeper secrets where humans have not even started to ask the right questions. Perhaps the universe is quite happy to keep things that way? However, we have come to that part in the story when we will discover a little bit more about how nature works that modern humans currently really cannot understand at all. Now we are about to find out just a little bit more about the nature of hidden spirits.

All of the world is full to overflowing with hidden spirits. Humans have some idea that there are things they cannot see and do not understand and they can call these ghosts or angels or prayers or fairies or intuitions or witches or dreams – really, they have all sorts of labels to try and explain things that they do not see or understand.

That's fine. The universe has seemed to have deemed it best to try and make sure that humans never get to understand these things because they will probably just come along with their greedy ways and mess things up for everything else.

The clouds do not want humans to know all the things that clouds do. Stars certainly do not want humans bothering them. Earthworms and butterflies and mountains and parsnips could all get along quite happily if humans were to suddenly disappear from the scene.

Humans like to think that they are important, they have been designed to think that way, however for everything else in the known and unknown universe humans are mostly irrelevant but occasionally quite bothersome. Sorry to tell you this, but you had to find out sometime.

Anyway, the reason that this is important is because we are nearing the place when the importance of the tarantulas and the jaguar and the sea eagle are going to get involved in what happens next, so you need to be forewarned about this.

Speaking of animal spirits; there is something of interest to say about young Grace. She comes from a part of Britain called Wales. This means that she is a Welsh person, as are her parents Steve and Katie.

Now all Welsh people have the spirit of the red dragon flowing through their blood. This is not one of those things that can be proven by science because there are no dragons around to take blood samples from. However, if you should ever be lucky enough to visit Wales then you will see that there are images of dragons everywhere.

There are flags of dragons on all the main buildings, there are statues of dragons on castles and in city halls and on lampposts. There are pictures of dragons on buses and trains and yet no-one alive has ever actually seen a dragon anywhere in the country at all.

So why do you think that is? Why do they not have mushrooms or goblins or cows dominating their landscape and cities? It is the passion and fire and wisdom and grandeur of the mighty dragon spirit that fills all the land and all of its people. It cannot be explained in a logical way in the manner humans might like. It is just a fact of the universe and simply the way things are. As the Welsh say, "get over it"!

This goes some way to explaining why Grace was able to cope so well when all those misfortunes we discussed earlier befell her. She is filled with the spirit of greatness. It is in her blood and in the air that she breathes when she is back home in Wales. The very air of the valleys is filled with kindness and song so those who live there just breathe it in without knowing.

We left our story at the most important point so far, even though it might not have seemed like it at the time. Quite simply, a previously silent young boy located somewhere beyond known civilization in the back of beyond was befriended by a small girl with her puppy and he then made a noise. So what? That really does not seem such a big a deal dos it?

Well, in actual fact humans have always failed to grasp the importance of small things like this. It was a very important thing indeed, as we shall see as our story progresses.

You have to understand that the very biggest and deepest oceans in all the world actually started as just one single droplet of water. In the same way the very biggest and most fearsomely solid mountain on any planet anywhere in the entire universe started as just one tiny little grain of sand. All of the light across all galaxies from every single Sun and star everywhere in the entirety of all of space and time began with the very first tiny spark that was spat out from the darkness.

So it is that everything that we might consider as big and important though our eyes and senses now all started off as something so tiny and insignificant that no-one would really notice if it happened right in front of them. That is another of those bigger mysteries of life we have been talking about.

So when the nameless and faceless boy squealed out aloud it was the calling point for the spirits who had been waiting in the darkness for eons to suddenly wake and take notice. What this noise turned out to be was a cry from the heart from that very last of the innocents. It was a call from that greatest spirit that we call nature into the air to all the creatures of the Earth and the spirits of the forests and the rivers and the mountains and the seas.

It was a cry out to the wider universe and through all of time that has been spent and that which humans call the future. It was a signal to the entire universe that the greed of humans has now gone too far. It was a call to arms for the spirits of those that care for nature to come together to prevent the onslaught that humans are inflicting on every single other atom and molecule on earth. It was a clarion call to say "enough is enough".

Far and wide the angels and the ghosts and the hidden things and the ancients and those that are deemed holy and those yet to come were alerted to the danger that is at hand.

All this simply because a brave girl called Grace was willing to play happily with a little boy who was different.

Grace and Reggie were totally oblivious to the wonderful thing they had unleashed. All they knew was that there was a little boy who seemed lonely and they wanted to play with him to cheer him up.

Soon the little boy, who had never had a play-mate before, began throwing sticks for Reggie to cheerfully chase and successfully capture and return to the thrower. Soon Grace was teaching him hop to play hop-scotch and catch chase.

Pretty soon the little boy with no face was running around and jumping and skipping and laughing and in no time at all he was no longer a miserable and sad and neglected little boy. He was becoming transformed into being a cheerful and lively lad with a new friend and a puppy to play with.

This also changed the people in the surrounds. They no longer avoided looking at the little boy but saw, some for the first time, that he existed. It was as if a magic spell of gloom had been lifted. Wherever Grace and Reggie were you could hear the sound of laughter and the occasional happy yap.

From nothing came sunshine and warmth. From grimness came joy. Grace did that just by simply being the lovely person that she was. It was a gift of joy that she had in her heart that she could share with the world.

Now humans can be as clever as they want but there are things they cannot explain, like where does laughter live before it is really to be heard? There are just so many mighty secrets to consider.

And so it was that Grace had completed her task. To her it was just a natural process that had required no thought. To those who engineer the workings of the universe it was the result of millions of years of intricate planning.

The boy had been made whole and now from the depths of the forest a new breath was set to energize the world. It was the kick start that was going to make humans think again. Just like the day when a girl called Greta elsewhere in the world one day decided that enough was enough.

All these small acts would help humans to think more seriously about the environment and there would be growing calls for the destruction to stop and better ways of living on the planet introduced.

However, with her part in the task completed Grace could not just be left alone in the forest with her family. The wisdom of the ancients knew that would just be wrong and so it was that a way to help them return home had been included in the master-plan. This involved the aid of other members of the task force. We have mentioned them already.

There were practical matters to take into consideration. Grace and Reggie and Steve and Katie had been saved from the isolation of their rough camps by the sides of the river, but they were still effectively lost in the desolate heartlands of the Amazon rain forest. No-one knew that this small settlement even existed and so no-one was going to come to take them back to more familiar surroundings.

The six toothless ancient ones had brought them this far: it seemed likely that they would continue to help the family on their journey, but that proved not to be the way things panned out. Remember, mighty forces are at play here and we come to the point where you have to consider other possibilities.

At least the Fyfe family were safe and had been able to feel rested and fed and watered, even if it was in the oddest place anywhere on the planet. Of course, no-one really spoke at all, and if they did it was not any kind of language that more worldly human types might use.

The oldest of the ancient ones gathered them together and gave them a handful of dried leaves as food for their onward journey and indicated that these should be chewed to give them strength. They tasted of dried tree bark and slightly bitter.

The oldest of the ancients then produced three tiny pieces of amber from his waistband and with a great level of solemnness in his bearing proceeded to give one each to Grace and her parents.

Now Grace was a girl who really loved collecting and playing with small things. At home her bedroom had lots of little pieces of jewelry and shiny small things. At Christmas and on her birthdays, she would always request that her gifts be tiny things rather than the bigger things that other, greedier types of children might ask for. That was just the way she was.

Grace was always a very grateful child, she had been brought up with excellent manners, and was really very thankful indeed to the old man for his kindness.

What Grace, nor her parents fully understood at this point is that they had been given precious "wonder stones". Remember we were still at a time when humans were ignorant of such things and had lost the ability to understand the deeper secrets of the Earth.

He then invited the three humans to sit and to close their eyes. It took a moment for the wonder stones to produce their magic, it had been so many thousands of years since they had last been used. For a moment nothing much happened and gradually the very oddest thing began to evolve. Into the mind of Steve and Katie and Grace emerged the image and voices of the Emperor and Empress of the tarantulas.

It was just so unbelievably weird having the thoughts and feelings of large spiders taking over your brain. It sounds a very scary thing to happen but it actually felt very natural indeed. Just like everything was meant to have happened this way.

The first thing to say is that tarantulas might seem very slow and calm sort of creatures but their brains really are not like that at all. Spiders have very twitchy brains and they are constantly looking around and checking out the smallest details and any changes or dangers or opportunities. Tarantulas are predictors and are really very good at what they do.

So having the spirit of a male and female spider running around in your head is one thing, but these two were just the absolute boss of all the spiders in all of the rain forest and so they were incredibly forceful.

The spiders indicated in the way that spirits communicate that they would be their guides for the first part of the journey to the nearest big village on the river where the family might be able to get help from their own kind.

The spiders said that they did not wish to be rude but that they had found humans to be quite disgusting and they were helping them not out of kindness but because they wanted them gone from the rain forest altogether. Sometimes bluntness is a good thing at other times is it simply just rude!

Grace felt a little bit aggrieved by these thoughts but Steve and Katie seemed to take it in their stride. After all, they just wanted to get out of this place too.

The tarantulas projected they would be guiding them through the underground tunnels to the edge of their territory and then the family would be passed on to another guide.

Now, this all sound completely and utterly mad, however, that is the way that animal spirits work. So you either accept it or you don't. That is just the way these things work.

The family wanted to thank the six ancient men for saving them but during the visitation from the spiders they had vanished back into the forest.

So tit was that two adults and a young girl and a puppy were led by the spirits of two spiders into the deeper passages that run far below the trees and the rivers and the hills and valleys of the Amazon basin.

There were no lights but spiders can see through the darkness of the cave passages and so none were needed. Animals are usually much better at this sort of thing than humans. Because the Emperor and Empress were so well respected all the other animals that might otherwise have enjoyed the prospect of helpless humans in their domain kept their distance and so no snakes approached them and no insects attacked them. The protected little group just marched and scrambled their way mile after mile though the blackness guided by the jittery demands of their distant hosts.

We know that the Bible is full of stories like this, Jonah being eaten by a whale or a worm being anointed or random people following instructions from dreams. None of this stuff is new, and yet people are less inclined to want to believe it since humans have decided that they are so much cleverer now. It's quite funny when you think about it.

So there we are Steve and Katie and Grace were all trundling along with a strong sense of where they were going. Poor Reggie had no idea what was happening. He just followed Grace faithfully like he always did. For, as you will appreciate, that was just his way.

Goodness alone knows how many miles they traversed though the blackness until, at last, the passageway emerged out through a small entrance back into the greenness of the forest and all the usual sounds and smells of the surface world.

Without saying any message of farewell or an opportunity for the family to say their thanks the spirit of the two tarantulas just dissolved way. It has to be said that spiders seem to have little time for manners, etiquette or the niceties of social interaction. They are a very direct and practical sort of animal and absolutely to be feared and not to be messed around.

So it seemed, on the surface at least, as if the little family were in an even worse position than they had been so many hours and hours ago when they had been in the settlement. Now here they were completely isolated without knowing where a river was as any kind of guide just completely surrounded by trees and the terrifying noises that echoed through the vines and darkness.

Deary, deary me. The little family were in a proper old pickle weren't they? So, what should they do now?

Chapter Eleven

ROUND AND POINTY THINGS

Another thing that most people do not really understand about rain forests until they are actually there is that it is actually quite rare to see the things that you think you will see. You know that the trees are full of animals, you can hear monkeys from miles away but they are very good at keeping themselves hidden. It is not often that you will come across a sloth even though they tend not to move around too much.

Then there are fruit-bats and pelicans and toucans and humming birds by the million but they keep themselves to themselves. On the ground there are no end of mice and guinea pigs and wild boar and armadillos and poisonous frogs and giant toads.

However, if you want to try and find one to even look at you need to be really very skilled, and our intrepid three travelers had not been trained in these things.

Another thing that you do not see much of is stone. The ground is made up of mud and stones and so there is plenty there, but the wild undergrowth and the leaves and low branches and endless growth of the flora of the world mean that every stone is covered by live or decaying organic matter. To see anything of stone is unusual, even the peoples who grow up in the darkest areas of the Amazon basin.

At the place where the family came out into the light there were stones just laying around on the floor of the canyon they found themselves in? Yet these were not like any other stones Grace or her parents had ever seen before. These were just random piles of perfectly round stones of different sizes.

There were hundreds of them just distributed in no describable pattern between the trees that had obviously grown up around them. The largest of the stones were about twelve feet in diameter and then all different sizes downwards with the smallest being about three feet across. Who had made them and why were they there? What a strange thing to find laying around in the middle of no-where.

Now we have already spoken a little bit about the deep mysteries of the universe. Sadly, humans have not yet fully understood about the nature of the universe and how time, wow! Now let us think for a minute about what we think we know. The planet Earth was formed and then along came all sorts of different animals and everything worked pretty well for millions of years. Then the way nature worked meant that living things all thrived and flourished and diversified and were all pretty happy and content with the way things were going.

Fish liked swimming, birds liked flying. Crawling creatures liked scrambling about and doing the sort of stuff that pleased them. The sun came up every day and everything was running along nicely. Different things happen at this time, some we think we know a little bit about, such as dinosaurs popping up and then disappearing, most things we do not know about because it has been agreed by those who know best that humans do not need to know. That's fine, no-one needs to know everything.

During this time there had always been fire. You know volcanoes were all over the place and made themselves known. The animals were wise enough to leave fire alone because it was known to be dangerous. But then humans came along and they could not help themselves, they just had to start playing with it and that is when things started to turn a bit ugly.

Do you remember that we found out that the biggest things start with the very smallest of actions? Well the moment the first human managed to work out how to move fire from one place to another was a pretty dark day for the rest of the planet.

Anyway, time passed by and humans suddenly changed from being quite irrelevant and useless creatures into something quite different. They started to find tools to use and they started to build things. Some people think that they did this all by themselves and other people think that they had help. It does not really matter how it happened. What matters to the Earth is that it did happen. Because humans that had appeared seemed to have been were made to be greedy. It just seems a simple flaw in their make-up. By and large most animals have some kind of behaviour trait that other species might not like, but for millions of year everything had just rumbled on happily together.

Then along came these greedy little creatures who started to take over the land that was used by others, and then chop down the trees that had been happily thriving all over the place. If you look at any map of the world today you can immediately see how the entire planet has changed just because some greedy new little species has plopped itself into the mix.

Anyway, the point is that there was a time when things were different. There was a time when the wonder stones were used and humans had been able to exchange themselves with the spirits of willing others. These giant round stones were remnant from that time. When the unknown history of the past of mankind had not yet been defined.

They were from a place before human greed got out of control. They can be found in unexpected locations all over the globe if anyone could be bothered to find out, but humans are too busy trying to get more and more things than they are to discover the hidden secrets. Perhaps it is best that things are kept that way.

In this most sacred and hidden place the family rested and wondered what would happen to them. Surely the staff of the Adventure magazine who had organized their competition holiday would have noticed that they were missing and search parties would have been sent out. However, they knew that they were well and truly lost and no-one in an airplane would ever be able to see through the green canopy of the forest to find out where they were.

Soon the family found some more stones and these were piled up on top of each other. They were very ancient and covered in vines. It seemed as if they were part of a pyramid, but that could not be right. What would a pyramid be doing here, so very far away from Egypt?
Not all humans know that pyramids can be found in all continents all over the world, because most people are just not interested enough in these things to find out. That is the way it is. Some would suggest that is almost certainly the way it was meant to be and is entirely for the best.

The three were not quite sure what to do next and it was Katie who suggested that perhaps the wonder stones might help. So they took out their little blocks of amber and a new animal spirit came into their minds to guide them. This time it was the mind of a jaguar.

Now it has to be said that jaguars think very differently to tarantula. Whereas spiders are really very jumpy and erratic the mind of any big hunting cat is exactly the opposite. It is very calm and measured and strongly reassuring. It has a great sense of power and is quite majestic in its sweep. It looks at a situation and will consider every single possibility before making a decision, and then it is explosive in its suddenness and furious.

For a human it is actually really very frightening to be seeing things through the eyes of a predatory large cat. However, jaguars are incredibly assured by the fact that all other animals are terrified of them and they prowl around in their own minds utterly without any fear at all.

At this point you might have started to want to know a little bit more about wonder stones. Well they are portals that do not have to be stones at all. In fact, amber is not a stone, it is actually a resin that sets almost as hard as stone.

Sometimes you can find small animals trapped inside resin and they are useful if you want to understand what it is like to be an insect or other tiny creature. Eventually humans will discover how to bring them back to life, but that is still quite a away into the future and we don't need to bother with that now.

So you know that there are all sorts of things that are not what they seem to be at all. For instance, a small oblong piece of paper can be just a useless scrap from a notebook or it can be a fifty-pound note and it then has extra meeting. A lump of metal can just be something found in a junkyard or it can be an ingot of gold and then humans get very excited about it.

You can say that water just looks like water, but it can also look like an ocean, or an iceberg or a cloud or steam. Most things are not what they seem and most things change. Beyond that there are those aspects of the universe that are hidden. Take for instance electricity. It has always been around since the start of the universe but animals and humans have only really found out about it very recently indeed.

You can see why a it was better for the world if such a power had remained secret, but it is the nature of all secrets that someday they will be revealed. We just have to hope that it is to the right sorts at the right time because misplaced power is a very difficult genie to get back in a bottle.

So it was the mind of the spirit of the jaguar had come to guide them back to the place where they belonged. You see Steve and Katie and Grace and Reggie all really belonged in Wales, it was all very nice for them to go off to see foreign lands and interesting places but there is something fundamentally important to remember and that is the value of "home".

There is nothing like being lost and abandoned in the Amazon rain forest to make anyone more focused on that particular lesson. What all of them would have given to be back in their garden watching Grace jumping about on her little trampoline?

So the spirit guided them slowly and deliberately up the difficult and gentle slopes of the stone pyramid. It took them slowly through the boughs of the trees where there were swarms of wasps and hornets and butterflies and crawling insects.

Now we all know that pyramids are fun. When you find out more about them you will discover that they almost always will have secret passages that run below them. Most of these have never been detected by humans but they will almost certainly be there. All across the world there are un-found structures that will have lakes of mercury below them and these have never been explained.

People try and work out how the size and location of a pyramid links in to the cosmology of the stars that float around millions of miles away in the night sky above them. They are almost always never, ever used as tombs, despite what the experts might tell you. These are all very interesting matters to some people while others just see a pointy building and do not think about them at all. That is just the way that some people are as the importance of the different things we encounter will differ with each and every soul on the planet.

In ordinary circumstances this would have been a really good opportunity to explore a previously undiscovered pyramid but the spirit of the jaguar was in charge of matters know and understood the severity of the situation the family were facing.

She wasted no time at all in instructing them to immediately direct their attention to securing safety for themselves. Her kind had been prepared for this role over many hundreds of thousands of years since the days when humans and animals were in complete harmony.

Long before they days when even this most ancient pyramid was started and the round stones so lovingly melded. This was part of the deeper mystery of destiny, and that is quite unfathomable to all, even those who created it.

The view from the top of the pyramid was not encouraging. All the humans could see were the tops of thousands and thousands of trees in all directions. There was no sign of any river or any mountain or escarpment. Just an endless vista of different shades of green and brown stretching out as far as their vision could extend. It looked endless and their cause seemed hopeless.

The spirit of the jaguar was quite unperturbed and directed them downwards to their left where the larger gaps in the encroaching greenery were fewest and the passageway a bit clearer for them. Grace found out that it is much quicker to travel down a pyramid than it is to go up it. Going up a pyramid you do not need a guide, travelling down one requires greater thought.

Who knows what treasures and secrets they might have discovered had they been able to stay among these wonderful stones but, it seemed that time was pressing and the jaguar felt that she needed them to make haste.

It very quickly became apparent that large female mammals are far more aware of their surroundings than arachnids, no matter how mighty their birth. The female jaguar seemed to sense the other animals of the rain forest for simply miles around. As the small party trudged on through the endless bushes and branches across a landscape that had no discernible tracks so she projected these thoughts into the minds of her new followers.

It seemed that there really were very many more dangers out there than any of the three humans had thought possible. They were all just hidden in their own secret places in the darkness just waiting and lurking or else seeking and stalking. It would have been overwhelmingly terrifying except that the calm assurance of the wonderfully sleek and powerful host managed to project a level of tranquility that seemed not just improbable, but utterly impossible.

So onward they stumbled, mile after green mile. Forcing their way through places where no human had ever stepped before travelling through a land that no human eye had ever even viewed before.

Now you might be thinking to yourself why it was that the wonder stones stopped being used and why it might be that humans decided to stop communicating in this way with the animals as it seems such a very good idea. Of course, that is not the way it worked.

What happened was that the animals one by one decided not to partake in the exchange of spirits anymore because they simply did not like what they saw in the minds of humans.

Animals have no need for names, they do not concern themselves in the business of others that does not concern them, and they have no interest in issues of greed and domination. Quite frankly they found humans to be pretty disgusting and one by one decided not to get involved with them. They hoped that humans would somehow just disappear.

The female jaguar had known from when she was a little cub that either she or one of her offspring would be the animal that would be chosen at this point in the spinning of the world to undertake this sacred duty. The child of man had completed her task of getting the mute faceless boy to cry out his alarm to the universe and it was her solemn duty to try and return her to the safety that she so richly deserved. You see, sometimes destiny in tainted with a trace of honour. The universe is not as soulless as some would paint it.

Of course the party were hungry. They had the strange leaves from the toothless men that gave them strength and occasionally the puma took them to edible plants that would cause them no harm. There was no actual water source to drink freely but remember it was a rain forest so they were all predominantly wet and able to survive. So it was that fruits and berries and soft nuts and pulpy grasses were the only options available,

After a number of days that seemed like an endless dream of trudging they party arrived at a place where a tiny spring of water could be seen leaking gently from the ground. It seemed that they had arrived at a place that was the source of one of the many such springs that would eventually be transformed into the greatest river the world had ever seen. It was one of those places that should remind us that very small any tiny things can become mighty.

Again, without a word of farewell the spirit of the jaguar just disappeared. She had performed with success the holy duty that she and all her family had been preparing for over millions of years. She could continue to stride with her calm pride in the knowledge that she had done well. She vowed to herself never to allow her spirit to enter the mind the mind of a human. What a terrifying place that is.

Chapter Twelve

CONTRADICTIONS

You know that they cannot teach you about the deeper mysteries at school. These are things that no-one can understand or agree upon – there is s clue in their name. These are the giant laws that forge our pathway from our very beginnings to the ultimate end of everything, if such a thing were ever to happen.

For the main part not knowing about them is a good thing. However, they will impact on every single life on the planet at every given moment and so they cannot be helped but be considered from time to time. There is one particular element that people will observe and never fully comprehend and that is the Secret law of Contradiction.

Perhaps the universe has a sense of humour or had been tainted by a spell of whimsy. Where it comes from is open to idle speculation however as sure as eggs is eggs, which is a pretty big assumption by the way, it is certain that in every single lifetime on the planet it will become obvious that some unseen mischief is at play.

It might be that the very worst person fit to run a country might become its leader. You will see that prizes for peace are given to people who conduct wars. People might win beauty prizes who are particularly ugly on the inside. These sorts of things happen every single day and it is not simply because of luck or mere chance.

Now as it happens Katie was just about the very fiercest Mother in all of Wales. In fact, if there had been a competition for the Mum who loved her child the most it might well have been won by her. She was also the most safety conscious person in the country. Grace was continually being told about the need to cross the road safely and to be aware of stranger danger and to be careful around hot things.

It was not that Katie was averse to danger but she was hugely protective and simply wanted the most precious thing in her life, which happened to be Grace, to be safe from harm. So it was a great prank from those who are responsible for the fate of human existence that it was Grace who was left isolated and lost on the wrong side of the Amazon River in the place that was farthest from all civilization on the continent. Someone or something somewhere was having a giggle about that.

You understand that Katie being so protective was just another way of her letting her daughter know that she loved her utterly. Grace was far from stupid, she already knew that.

In a slightly different way, Grace really loved Reggie and the small puppy understood that and was utterly devoted to his young companion. Reggie loved just being next to her and would happily spend all his time running around her feet or sitting on her lap or sleeping by her side. They were devoted to each other. He was not the sort of small dog who would just rush off and be distracted by the things of the undergrowth and that was just as well because there were things out there that were dangerous.

In fact, it seems really very strange indeed that none of the small party of adventurers had actually been hurt by anything in the wild so far. They had fallen in the river and had not been swallowed underneath the heavy brown water. They had not been attacked by piranhas or crocodiles or cayman or electric eels whilst swimming and scrambling through the murk to the shore.

They had not been attacked by the millions of insects that surrounded them, or poisoned by the bright green frogs that lived where they had camped. The various snakes and spiders that they had disturbed had observed them all of the time but had left them alone. They had not been particularly badly scratched by the thorny undergrowth or fallen over all the things that trip you up as you try to pass through the deepest thickets.

The larger animals who might usually have fancied a little bit of human for dinner had all known they were there but had not bothered to even begin to try and eat them. It was as if the rain forest were actually protecting them – which, of course, it was.

You see, nearly always divine secrets have mysteries hiding within mysteries which are camouflaged and disguised from the original mystery itself. It is almost as if mysteries might come in pyramid forms, what do you think? It is just an idea.

So now we come to the place where the third guide takes over the duty guiding Steve and Katie and Grace and little Reggie back home and, as you might anticipate, it came in the form of a contradiction.

There is no way that a sea eagle would normally be seen this far inland. Yes, there is a clue in the name. Sea eagles tend to operate over salty waters on the coast or even further out into the wider oceans.

You can live a thousand years and never again be able to view a sea eagle this far inland. However there she was, high in the sky and imperious using her simply amazing vision to seek out the straggling wanderers on their long trek through this geographical void.

From her lofty vantage point high in the clear bright sky above she could finally see the small party of humans with their silly fluffy brown companion bending down into the earth and using their claw-less hands to cup water to drink from. She had always thought that claw-less hands would be pretty useless but this seemed like a good idea.

She cast her spirit into the minds of the humans and, just like the spiders and the jaguar before her, she was utterly repulsed by the chaos and levels of strangeness they had to cope with.

Why on earth did humans have to bother themselves with so very much that had nothing to do with them? Why did they collect so many useless things? What was all this madness that they called money? Why didn't they want to know about all the important things? Why couldn't they see all the harm that they were doing and stop it?

It was then that the sea eagle discovered that humans actually did know that they were causing irreparable harm to the planet but it seemed, many of them just really didn't care at all. How shocking! She was suddenly very glad indeed that she was a sea eagle and could very literally rise herself away from such terribleness.

She immediately realized that this was going to be a much more difficult task than she had imagined. Not because she felt that her role was too difficult, all she had to do was find them a path to the nearest settlement, but because she would have to try and work her way through all these strange concepts that seemed to consume humans.

Steve and Katie and Grace were all very nice people. It was not their fault that they had been born into humanity. In fact, it was because Grace had been the one selected by the universe to wake the faceless boy that she was so very special and needed the help of the spirits of the Amazon. No, it was just so disturbing to see how very different these creatures were from all the other animals that she had come across in her time as a sea eagle.

In fact, she had always felt that her way of life was pretty good. It helped that she really liked eating fish. Had she not have found fish quite so delicious then being a sea eagle might not have been quite so good. So the universe had worked that out very well for her and she was grateful. The fish probably had a different viewpoint.

So the sea eagle had flown for over a thousand miles inland to the place where one of the small tributaries of the Amazon oozed from the complex waterways below the surface of the world into the light and air of an entirely new domain. Every single drop of water on a journey that would end up who knows where?

For some it would mean passing through the belly of the happy little puppy that seemed to have been given a name. Other drops of water would end up in the ocean a thousand miles away, others would be taken up into the sky and scuttle along as clouds before falling to earth and then who knows what? The way of nature is wondrous and marvelous and it is not the place of a sea eagle to do anything other than to rejoice at how incredible this planet is.

Next began the third experience where the "wonder stones" helped Grace and her little band onward a place where their rescue could be properly concluded. The sea eagle knew well enough that if her humans just followed the course of the water in its pathway through the trees and valleys then it would turn from a trickle to a steam and gradually gain strength.

Then it would grow gradually busier and busier until it fulfilled its function as a tributary and joined its brothers and sisters to become a part of the little river that would, in turn, grow bigger and bigger and become the fabulous monster that humans had called the Amazon river. All they had to do was keep following the flow of the water. How hard could that possibly be?

Well, these were humans. It seems that nothing is easy where these most strange of animals are concerned. At first it was pretty straightforward. Steve and Katie and Grace all seemed to understand what the sea eagle was instructing them, even though she was very many miles away in a physical sense.

Sea eagles are not accustomed to being that far inland and she was a little bit unsure about the terrain down there. She had never actually been inside a rain forest before, just flown high above and observed the goings on from a distance.

Anyway. It seems that the way springs from the ground is not quite as simple as you would think. Firstly, there is one over there and then it disappears underground and then another one pops up nearby and seems to go in a different directions. So at first the little family and their puppy could be viewed going from spring to spring and seeming to trace back on themselves. From the sky it seemed like they were just walking around in circles!

The sea eagle realized that she needed to get a bit closer in order to better direct them, even though it went against her better judgment. Given that she too was so far from home and also a little bit scared it was a very brave thing to do.

So it was that she flew to where the family were struggling to make sense of things and landed atop the highest of the trees. She had imagined that this would be a place devoid of all life and was really surprised to discover that virtually every single twig and leaf had little animals just living their lives so very high in the air.

It took a while for the minds of Katie, Steve and Grace to get used to the very different way a bird thinks. It really is completely different from the twitch of the spiders or the calm assurance of the puma. The sea eagle is somehow more detached and dreamlike. She held her thoughts in a savage floating whisper. It was as if someone were trying to eat a dream. She was calling out "tun left now", The family turned right. It was really frustrating for her.

However, after a couple of hours things sorted themselves out. We live in a universe where problems always seem to get themselves resolved.

She tried hard not to think too much about fish, but the more she tried to focus on the family below her the more her mind seemed to want to think about her proper place by the sea. Apparently, there are lots of birds who find it hard to concentrate and it appears that sea eagles are one of these.

So this transfer of spirits did not start off too well but. like all things, a balance was eventually found and the family were soon back on the right track. They were heading down the tributary and knew that they would eventually find themselves in a place where the River Amazon would once again be in sight.

It was actually quite a few more days before that particular reunion happened. In the meantime, a different type of incident interrupted the smooth running of proceedings.

As we have discussed the sea eagle was very easily distracted. As the waterways below got gradually wider so it was that they became more likely to be3come the home to fish. We have established that this particular bird was especially fond of fish. So it was that one morning she swooped down with her usual precision and was able to spear a medium sized specimen for her breakfast. This is natural and the way of wild things.

However, the sea bird was not used to freshwater fish and this specific one was poisonous to sea eagles. So that was not good. Not good at all.

The sea eagle very quickly became very ill and became quite delirious. Not having the spirit of a fit and healthy bird guiding you through the most dangerous terrain on the plant is one thing. Having to follow the instructions of a bird that is filled with sickness and madness is quite another.

It was Katie who was first to understand what was happening and she instructed the crazed giant bird to come to her to see if she could assist in any way. So it was that a giant sea eagle came tumbling through the trees and bushes and landed in the water beside the little family. Katie and Steve tried to reassure and comfort the terrified bird.
However, it was little Reggie who really came to the rescue. Because the family were suddenly at rest after so many days and endless toil of trekking the small brown puppy thought it was time to play. He went charging around the little river and found a place where he could actually quite easily catch fish. He very proudly would deliver them to Grace as presents of love. That is just the way puppies are!

Now these little fish were not poisonous to sea eagles and so Katie and Steve were able to slowly help bring the sea eagle through its time of sickness and she gradually felt that her health was being restored. All this all sounds quite simple but it was more difficult than you might imagine. Having the wildly bizarre thoughts of a deranged sea eagle eating away in your head is a far from happy experience.

As the sea eagle slowly recovered she understood that there is a deep kindness in humans and she was not as entirely repulsed by them as she had been previously. She still found them pretty disusing, but not quite as entirely awful as she had previously thought.

The sea eagle found that she actually really liked quite a lot about Katie in particular. She really admired how her quiet fierceness and love burned through her. She knew that she would never want to be in an argument with her, yes indeed, that little human was fierce. A bit too much dragon blood in there perhaps?

As predicted as each mile went by so the river got gradually wider and wider and faster and faster. It was at this point that Steve decided that it might be worthwhile considering making a raft. The entire party were completely fatigued. It is no easy thing traipsing for mile after mile through heavy undergrowth and thick forest, no matter how protected you might be.

As you can guess, none of them had ever actually even attempted to make a raft before. Just how difficult can it be? Well, as it happens, if you have never done it before the entire business of raft making can actually be quite problematic altogether.

Everyone scouted around looking for suitable logs or branches that could be used for the venture. Now even though they were surrounded by millions and millions of trees for hundreds of miles in all directions it seemed that there were only three actual branches in the entire forest were going to be available for them. Then how do you join them all together?

Although there were all manner of thick vines surrounding them it seemed that there was nothing in this particular area that would do the trick. After quite a few hours embarking on this enterprise they had managed to create something that looked as much like a rough sort of raft as anything could.

The family all tried to get on it but it either sank or fell apart within moments, so they tried and tried again. Far above in the highest tree a misplaced recovering sea eagle was looking down utterly bemused. Her recent madness was nothing in comparison to this.

Finally, things started to come together. They had worked out a way of getting the raft to work. Not all of them could sit on it at the same time but Grace could balance on the branches and her parents could float alongside and grip the sides. As long as the waters were not too busy this would work, but as soon as there was any major ripple in the surface the raft became unsafe.

To some degree it worked and for a number of miles the journey down the river was much faster even though it was often very uncomfortable and perhaps even more dangerous. It was certainly a lot wetter.

They had not thought they could get any wetter, but traveling on a makeshift raft on a flowing river makes you just about as wet as you can possibly be. Luckily all three of them were excellent swimmers and even Reggie could manage to keep his head above water when he needed to.

Up above the sea eagle would go soaring high to find out when this growing tributary would find its path to the main course way that would meander so majestically and timelessly across the continent towards its massive delta ending.

Eventually, in the very far distance she saw that familiar trace of thick brown lurching on the horizon. In the immediate path the sea eagle saw a couple of things that she knew were going to be problems. Animals do not have a word for them but humans call them rapids and waterfalls.

So it was that Grace was suddenly rushing on a couple of loosely tied branches rushing headlong into the white and dangerous waters as the fast flowing waters raged all around her.

Suddenly things felt very different. She could actually feel wetness. It was no longer imagined or dreamlike. This was real there was wetness on her face and she felt the shock of this coldness and new sensation. What was happening now?

Chapter Thirteen

HOME

In his usual happy way Reggie had jumped up onto her bed and was licking her face. This is the way that Grace woke up every morning. It was one of the very favourite parts of her day.

What a strange dream she had had. As you know very often you can wake up in the middle of a story and start to wander what the ending might be but, as your waking mind starts to focus on the real world around you, the memory of what you have been thinking can vanish in a gentle flash.

So it was with Grace. Had the events been happening for real she would have wanted to know if they had ever managed to get to a village on the river. Then how would the family have been able to return from the depths of deepest Brazil back over the oceans and happily returned to their house in Wales.

However, it is the nature of wakefulness that such things just melt into insignificance and the practicalities of getting up and brushing teeth and hair and putting on clothes somehow just take over. All creatures follow daily routines and this story has reminded us that humans are animals too.

When she pulled the curtains it seemed as if it might be quite a sunny day outside. Reggie was already very excitedly wagging his little tail and ready to have some food. Katie and Steve were already in the kitchen pouring out cereals into a bowl and a kettle had already been boiled. It was just another normal morning in the Fyfe household and it seems as if the adventures of the night had never really happened after all.

Perhaps some people would say that is the way of dreams. Others might suggest that having a happy breakfast with people you love in a place where you feel safe with a happy puppy by your side is just another example of those great secret mysteries of the universe that humans just take for granted.

When you come to think about it, the fact that a lovely eight-year-old girl called Grace Fyfe is a small part of immense and magnificent universe is just a wonderful mystery all on its own. Don't you think?

ABOUT THE AUTHOR

David Hiscox lives in Cardiff, Wales.
He has two step children, Becky and James,

OTHER BOOKS BY THIS AUTHOR

Fiction

THE "LITTLE KIT" SERIES:-

Book 1   CAMOUFLAGE
         by Little Kit (pseudonym for David Hiscox)

Book 2   SUBTIFUGE
         by Little Kit

Book 3   CABBAGE
         by Little Kit

Book 4   CHOP!
         by Little Kit

Book 5   SAUSAGE
         by Little Kit

Book 6   THE STRANGE SIXTH BOOK
         by Little Kit and David Hiscox

         MR HANKS IS MISSED
         By David Hiscox

Children's books

AMAZONIAN GRACE
by David Hiscox

THE SHADOW FAIRY
by David Hiscox

All available on Amazon Publishing and Kindle audio-book.

Printed in Great Britain
by Amazon

27712843R00046